BABY ZEKE

The diary of a chicken jockey

Book 2 – Into the Mine

(an unofficial Minecraft book)
(Baby Zeke Book 2)

By,
Dr. Block

Published by Eclectic Esquire Media, LLC
P.O. Box 235094
Encinitas, CA 92023-5094

Inquiries and Information: *drblockbooks@gmail.com*

TABLE OF CONTENTS

Chapter 1

I stared at the point of the ultra-sharp diamond sword held in the hand of the baby zombie pigman. It was only inches from my neck.

"Cat got your tongue?" he snarled at me.

"What?" I whimpered.

"I asked you a question," he said. "What are you doing in my cave?"

I glanced over at my chicken, Harold. He was petrified. I had to say something.

"Well, we were just looking for a place to hide during the day, and we found this place so we thought we'd stay, at least for a little while."

The baby zombie pigman laughed. "Yeah, right. You're here to take this place from me, aren't you?"

"We didn't even know it was your place, so how could we want to take it from you?" I asked.

"Shut up," he said, pushing the sword closer to me. "You know it's mine now."

"That's true," I said in as calm a voice as I could manage, hoping the baby zombie pigman would relax a bit.

Our captor backed away a few feet and then motioned with his sword to the cave's exit. "Get out," he said.

"But, it is still daylight. There are probably players roaming around. You can't make us go out there," I implored him.

He chuckled. "I can do whatever I want. I have the

diamond sword, remember?" To emphasize his point he jumped at me and waved the tip of his sword a few inches from my nose.

"You're not very nice," said Harold.

The baby zombie pigman shot him an icy stare. "I don't need to be nice to stay alive," he growled. "Get out!"

"Let's go, Harold. We'll find someplace else," I said sadly. I picked up my sack of beef and wheat that Zeb had given me before our exile from the zombie horde and began walking to the exit of the cave.

As Harold and I shuffled toward the exit of the cave, Harold looked up at me and said, "It's okay. There are still a few hours of daylight left. We can find a new cave before the sun sets."

I reached over and patted Harold's neck. "I hope so."

Then, just as we were about to leave the cave, we heard a loud clucking behind us and then someone said, "Harold? Is that you?"

Chapter 2

Harold and I turned around and saw a chicken standing next to the baby zombie pigman.

"Bob?" said Harold. "Is it really you?"

"Yes!" clucked the other chicken excitedly.

Harold and Bob rushed together, reached their wings around each other and exchanged a long bro hug.

"I thought you were dead," said Harold, a little tear of joy running from one eye.

"Same here," said Bob.

As they pushed away from their bro hug, the baby zombie pigman said to Bob, "Wait. You know these guys?"

Bob nodded. "Yes. Well, I know Harold anyway. I don't know the baby zombie."

"His name is Zeke," said Harold. "He helped me save some of our friends who got captured by villagers."

"Hi, Bob," I said, waving my hand.

"Hi, Zeke."

The baby zombie pigman slapped his face with his hand. "Seriously? I act all crazy and scare these guys away from the cave and you know one of them?"

I walked over to the baby zombie pigman and said, "Forget about it."

"Sorry," he said.

"Don't worry about it," I said. "What's your name?"

"Otis."

I extended an undead hand and Otis reached his out. We shook hands. "Nice to meet you,"

I said. "And, it's nice not to have a sword pointed at my face."

Otis looked embarrassed. "Yeah, well, there are lots of bad mobs out there. I was just being safe. Me and Bob had to go through a lot to survive and find a place like this. I wasn't going to allow any chicken jockey to take it from us."

"Sure," I said. "I totally understand." I paused for a moment and then asked, "So, are you a pigman jockey?"

Otis nodded, "Yes, sir."

"Cool," I said. "We should start a jockey gang."

Otis rolled his undead eyes. "Oh, please, can we?" he said sarcastically.

"I was kidding," I said. "Anyway, how did you get to the Overworld? Shouldn't you be in the Nether?"

Otis seemed sad for a moment, and then said, "It's a long story. I don't want to talk about it."

I looked down at the diamond sword in Otis's hand. *What is a baby zombie pigman doing with a diamond sword?*

"How did you get that awesome sword?" I asked.

Otis looked over at Bob and raised an eyebrow. Bob nodded and said, "Show them."

"Follow me," said Otis.

Chapter 3

Otis led us across the large cavern in which we had been standing toward a narrow passage. He grabbed a torch from the wall and told us each to grab one.

"It's a pretty long walk from here," said Otis. "Be sure to watch your step."

As we walked through the narrow passage, I said to the chickens, "What did you mean back there about thinking you were both dead?"

Bob sighed. "Well, Harold and I were part of a large group of chickens, maybe fifteen of us, right Harold?"

"Sounds about right," said Harold.

"Anyway, we were minding our own business, scratching the ground for seeds when a wolf arrived and ate one of us."

"Rest in peace, Glenda," said Harold softly.

Bob nodded. "We all panicked and ran in all directions. As we ran, another couple of wolves arrived and started eating more chickens. We all had to scatter if we had any hope of survival. That was the last I saw of Harold. I met Otis the next day."

"You know those chickens we freed back in the village?" said Harold.

I nodded.

"They were with that group. A few of us managed to get back together after the wolf attack, but we just assumed all the other chickens were dead."

"Intense," I said.

After that sad tale, we walked silently for a time, still in single-file behind Otis in the narrow passageway. In some spots, the passage was barely one block wide and we had to move quite slowly.

After a few more minutes, the passage started to become wider and wider as it slowly opened into a large chamber.

"Here we are," said Otis.

We had entered a broad chamber, probably fifty blocks wide and eight blocks high. A small underground creek gurgled slowly through the center of the chamber. There was a small lava pit in one corner of the chamber.

"I bet there are lots of valuable ores near," I said.

"Yep," said Otis. "I've done a little mining and found some pretty awesome stuff, even some redstone ore and diamond ore."

"So, you made the sword yourself?" I asked, totally impressed.

Otis shook his head. "No. I'll show you."

Otis led us to a cobblestone wall. He pulled a pickaxe from his inventory and quickly knocked away four blocks. Behind them was a chest.

"I was mining a few days ago and came across this chest hidden behind several layers of stone. My guess is some player hid it in here long ago."

"Whoa," I said.

"Cool," said Harold.

"Yeah, it is," Otis continued. "When I opened it up, I found all sorts of awesome stuff in it, including this diamond sword. There's also all sorts of potions, armor and other weapons."

"Can I open it?" I asked.

"Sure," said Otis. "Why don't you pick out some more weapons so you have something more than just your iron sword?"

I rushed over to the chest and opened it. I had never seen so many amazing things in one location: swords, bows, axes, armor, potions and even a book labeled *Steve's Diary*.

"Wow!" I exclaimed.

Otis smiled. "Pretty awesome, huh?"

"It sure is," I said as I grabbed a bow and ten arrows from the chest. "Too bad there isn't another diamond sword," I muttered.

"I got the only one," said Otis, slashing his gleaming sword through the air and smiling like a madman … er … mad-zombie.

I rummaged further through the chest. "Any baby-sized armor in here?" I asked. "This leather armor is pretty weak."

"No, nothing," said Otis. "I need some armor myself."

I picked up *Steve's Diary* and said to Otis, "You read this yet?"

He laughed. "Of course not. Who would want to read someone else's diary?"

I shrugged. And then opened the diary and started reading: "It was the best of times, it was the worst of times, it was the age of wisdom, it was the age of foolishness, it was the epoch of belief, it was the epoch of incredulity, it was the ..." *What the heck?* I put the diary back in the chest.

I looked through the potions and grabbed a potion of healing, of strength and a splash potion of harming. "You never know when these might come in handy," I said to Otis.

"Agreed," he replied.

I looked at the chickens. "I don't see anything in the chest you guys might like. No grains of any kind."

"That's okay," said Harold. "Chickens are used to having to scratch the ground to find their food."

Chickens sure are accepting of their lot in life, I thought.

I made one last scan of the chest and was about to close it when a small bottle tucked in the back corner of the chest caught my eye. I reached down and lifted the bottle.

"Oh my gosh," I said, "a potion of invisibility!"

"No way. How did I miss that?" asked Otis, who sounded a little jealous.

"It was hidden under some sheets of paper," I said, trying not to gloat about my awesome find.

"Keep it handy. You never know when you might need it to get away from a player," said Otis.

I nodded my agreement and then yawned. "Otis, man, I'm tired. You wouldn't happen to have any beds around here?"

Otis grinned. "Come with me."

Otis led us down another narrow passage that was only about ten blocks long before it opened up into a cozy room. Inside the room were three beds and a nest made of sticks. The walls were decorated with pictures in item frames and there were glowing torches on the walls.

"Nice," I said. "Did you craft all of this?"

"It was like this when we found it," said Otis. "All I needed to do was light the torches."

I whistled. "Someone worked pretty hard on this cave. Hiding a chest full of loot and building this room."

"There is also a deep mine down another passage," said Bob.

"Really?" I said.

I was starting to get worried. If a player – maybe that Steve guy who left the weird diary – built all this, he was sure to return. And, he would not like us being here.

"Aren't you afraid that whoever built this is going to come back?" I asked Otis. "I mean, if he is leaving diamond swords and bottles of potions laying around, he is probably pretty dominant. He might even have enchanted weapons."

Otis did not seem too concerned. "This cave is huge. We'd hear anyone coming – like I heard you – and be able to escape before anything bad happened."

Otis seemed to have it all worked out, so I said, "Sounds good to me."

After that, we sat down and ate dinner and then got in to bed. Bob gave Harold some of his sticks to use as a nest.

We were all just drifting off to sleep when we heard and felt a massive explosion from deep inside the cave.

Chapter 4

Otis jumped out of bed and lit a torch. "Is everyone okay?" he asked. We all were fine, just frightened.

"It sounded like it came from below us," I said.

Otis nodded. "Yeah, I think it came from deep inside the mine. Maybe the main mine pit."

"Do you think someone is down there?" I asked.

"Could be," said Otis. "Or, it could be that some lava dripped on some TNT blocks and set off an explosion. The only way to be sure is to go down there and check it out."

"Ugh," I grunted. "I guess sleep will have to wait."

Otis turned to Bob and Harold and said, "It is a pretty steep, narrow path through the mine, so we should probably ride you guys."

"No problem," said Bob.

"Sure," said Harold.

Otis and I climbed aboard and got comfortable in our jockey

positions. I still felt a little bad about riding Harold, but we made a great team and we could maneuver much more quickly when I was sitting on him.

"Let's move out," said Otis. "And, let's try to be as quiet as possible. We don't know who or what might be down there."

The rest of us nodded our assent. Then, Otis and Bob took the lead, while Harold and I followed.

We passed through the short narrow exit from the sleeping chamber into the larger chamber where I had searched the chest.

Then, we went to another crack in the wall, almost unnoticeable until I was just a few blocks away from it.

We entered the new crack and had to walk single-file for quite some time. I was starting to feel a little claustrophobic, trying to do some deep breathing exercises to stay calm.

"Are you alright?" whispered Harold.

"Fine, I think," I whispered back. "I just hope we get into a larger space soon."

Fortunately, it wasn't much longer until we entered an

expansive chamber carved out of cobblestone.

"The entrance to the mine," said Otis, sweeping his little arm across the panorama.

"Whoa," I said. "This room is huge. It's only the *entrance*?"

"Yeah, this mine is enormous. Someone or some group spent a lot of time mining here," said Otis. "And, I can understand why. I've only been mining for a little while, and I've found quite a bit of diamond ore."

"Cool," I said.

Otis pointed across the room and said, "The rest of the mine is through that opening and down. I'm sure the explosion happened down there somewhere."

"Let's go," said Harold.

The path into the depths of the mine was surprisingly organized. Whoever had created the mine would go down a few blocks, then branch out in a pattern searching for ore on each level. After the level had been explored, the miner had returned to the main path, dug down a few more blocks, and then would repeat the branching pattern.

"Great design," I whispered.

"Yeah, and it will make it easy to see where the explosion occurred," said Otis.

He was right. A huge hole blown in the earth would be a stark contrast to the almost geometric design of the mine.

A little while later, we were just getting ready to descend to a new level when I heard some skittering noises followed by hissing.

"Something's coming," I whispered to Otis as I drew my sword.

Otis drew his sword too. Then, we told Bob and Harold to

back us into opposite corners and hide until we could see what was coming. Otis and Bob were on one side of the passage, while Harold and I were on the other.

We waited just a few seconds until a pack of six cave spiders came up from the level below. *Six?* I thought. *This was going to be a tough battle.*

"Okay, Harold," I whispered into Harold's ear hole. "When I kick my feet against you, jump in front of the lead spider. Let's hope Otis and Bob follow our lead."

"Got it," responded Harold.

I waited until just the right moment and then kicked Harold. He moved swiftly in front of the lead cave spider who hissed with surprise.

I raised my sword, ready for battle.

Chapter 5

I brought my sword down with all my might, hoping to slice the lead spider in half, sending shock and awe through the remaining spiders, making them easier to kill.

But, instead of striking spider flesh, my sword hit diamond, making a *cha-PING* sound as it bounced off.

"No!" yelled Otis, as he extended his sword in front of

mine just in the nick of time, stopping my attack.

All the spiders hissed and surrounded me. *Just great*, I thought.

"I know these guys," said Otis. "They're cool."

"You could have let me know you had friends down here," I said, putting my sword away.

The lead spider looked at Harold and me with his eight red eyes and hissed, "You are lucky you are with Otis, chicken jockey, or your fate would have been death."

"Whatever," I said, trying to act like he hadn't completely terrified me. I could feel Harold shivering with fear below me.

"Stop it, you two," said Otis.

"No hard feelings?" I said to the spider.

"None," hissed the spider. "The world is a dangerous place."

"So, Beegu," Otis said to the lead spider, "do you or your people have any idea what that explosion was?"

"No, I do not," said Beegu. "We were just wandering through the mine when we heard it. It was huge, and the ground started shaking. It even broke some rock loose around us."

"We felt it in my sleeping chamber too," said Otis.

"I decided we needed to move higher in the cave," said Beegu. "In fact, if the explosions continue, we may wait until night fall and then move to a safer cave."

"Have you noticed anything else unusual in the past few days?" I asked.

"Nothing other than I thought I smelled zombies yesterday," said Beegu. "I thought that was odd because the only time I ever smell zombie this deep in the mine is when you are down here, Otis."

Otis and I looked at each other. Why would a zombie be so far down in the mine? Zombies prefer to stay on the surface near villages.

"Weird," said Otis. "Maybe you smelled something else?"

"Maybe, but I doubt it," said Beegu.

"Thank you, Beegu, for the information. We are going to go deeper to see if we can determine what the explosion was," said Otis.

"Suit yourselves," said Beegu. "But, for what it's worth, you are going the wrong direction."

We watched as Beegu and his group went on their way, their many legs moving up and down like pistons.

"Spiders freak me out," said Harold.

"I know what you mean, buddy," I said.

"Quit your whining and let's get going," said Otis. "We need to figure this out."

We continued further down the mine, Otis leading the way. We had walked for a few minutes when we started to hear faint noises coming from somewhere down in the mine. The noises sounded like plinking or scraping sounds, but they were so far away it was difficult to be certain.

"Maybe pickaxes on stone?" I suggested.

"Maybe," said Otis. "But, it sounds like a lot of them. I can't believe an entire group of people got past me."

"Maybe they came in some other way," said Harold.

"What do you mean?" asked Otis.

"They could have started mining somewhere else and just ended up here," explained Harold.

"I never thought of that," said Otis. "Maybe you are correct."

"Makes sense to me," said Bob.

"Well, we will never find out just sitting here theorizing about it," said Otis. "We need to get down there quickly."

"I'm hungry," said Bob.

Otis let out an exasperated sigh. "Fine, let's stop and eat for a few minutes. But make it quick."

After we finished eating, we continued down the mine. The noises were getting louder and louder the deeper we went. I was starting to get very nervous.

"Sounds like a lot of things moving around down there to be making so much noise," I said to Otis.

Otis nodded his agreement. "We are getting close," he said.

"Do you really think this is a good idea?" I asked. "I mean, it is probably a bunch of players down there. We won't stand a chance against them."

"Don't be such a wimp," said Otis. "Besides, if there are too many of them, we can run away and blow up some TNT traps I've set. It would take them days to mine through the rubble. They would never find us."

I had to admit, I was impressed that Otis had already set TNT traps throughout the mine. But then, what if the people making all the noise had done the same thing?

We walked for a few more minutes, the noises getting louder and louder. Finally, it sounded like they were only a few feet away.

It was then that we noticed a huge gash torn in the cobblestone. There were piles of rubble scattered across the path.

"This must be where the explosion happened," whispered Otis as he dismounted from Bob and told me to get off Harold.

We followed Otis as he crept slowly forward to a low pile of rocks. "It sounds like the noises we heard are coming from in there," he said quietly. "Let's take a look."

We all slowly raised our heads over the rubble to look.

What I saw chilled me to my little undead core.

Chapter 6

At the bottom of the giant pit created by the explosion, I saw ten zombies chained together. They each held a pickaxe and were slowly mining. Behind the enslaved zombies stood two players.

The players looked very dominant. Each was wearing full diamond armor and they held diamond swords.

"Keep digging, you filthy zombies," yelled one of the players.

"Yeah, we need to extract all the good ore from this mine as soon as possible, before Steve comes back," added the other player.

They know about Steve, too! He must have really built all of this and left his diary and weapons in that chest for safekeeping.

I felt sorry for the captured zombies, forced to labor against their will on behalf of these greedy players. Then, I looked more closely at the pathetic captured zombies and recognized Zeb among them!

I sat down behind the pile of rocks. "No," I said softly. "No, no."

"What is it?" whispered Otis.

"One of the captured zombies is my friend, Zeb," I explained.

"That's lame," said Otis.

I looked at Harold. "We have to save him, Harold. He was the only one who stood by us when we were with the other horde."

Harold nodded. "Yes, we should. But how?"

"Are you guys crazy?" asked Otis. "Didn't you see those dominant griefers down there? We can't defeat those guys."

"What's a griefer?" I asked.

"Seriously? Are you a noob?" asked Otis.

I frowned. "Just tell me."

"A griefer is a player who likes to destroy the work of other players. Obviously, they found out Steve had created this mine and wanted to destroy it, but not until they first steal everything of value."

"That's terrible," said Harold. "Why would anyone want to do that?"

Otis shrugged. "Who knows?"

"If they are griefing Steve's mine, does that mean Steve is alive and he might come back?" asked Bob, trembling.

Otis rubbing his chin, thinking. "Gee, Bob, it might. I think we should get out of here and find a new place to live. I don't want Steve to find us and think we griefed his stuff. I've heard Steve is pretty powerful."

"So, you just want to abandon my friend down there?" I asked Otis.

"What choice do we have? We can't face those griefers," said Otis.

I sat there feeling sad. I couldn't just abandon my friend. Harold came over and put a wing on my shoulder, trying to comfort me. And then, I had an idea.

"What if we don't have to face them?" I said.

"What do you mean?" asked Otis.

"I have that potion of invisibility. Maybe I can drink it and sneak down there undetected and free Zeb," I said.

Otis shook his head. "That won't work. Suddenly Zeb is walking around free. What then? The griefers will just grab him again and you will have wasted your potion."

I did not want to admit it, but Otis was right. It would be futile.

I was ready to give up hope and leave Zeb to his fate, when Harold said, "I think I have an idea."

Chapter 7

We talked through Harold's idea, and thought it just might work. It would be risky, but I couldn't just leave Zeb there to suffer. Even Otis realized it was the right thing to do and agreed to help.

"Ready?" asked Harold. We all nodded our silent assent. Seeing that we were ready, Harold turned and began walking. We watched as he disappeared into a crack.

A few moments later, we heard one of the griefers say, "Hey, look at that. A chicken!"

"How did a chicken get so far down in the mine?" asked the other griefer.

"Who knows," said the first griefer. "He probably just got lost. Chickens are so stupid."

The griefers laughed. Then one said, "Let's kill it and eat it."

That was my cue. I quickly drank the potion of invisibility and snuck through the same crack Harold had used. When I entered the mine pit, I saw Harold running from one of the griefers.

"Come back here, you stupid chicken and let me kill you!" said the griefer chasing him.

"Ha! Ha! You can't even catch a dumb chicken," said the other griefer.

While Harold kept the first griefer busy, I took out my splash potion of harming and snuck behind the laughing griefer. I stood as close to him as I could and whispered, "Boo."

"What?" said the griefer as he turned around quickly. Seeing nothing, the griefer said in a panicky voice, "Who .... who's there?"

As he was looking at me, I tossed the splash potion in his face and said, "Drink up, griefer."

"Ahhhhhhhhhh," screamed the griefer. "Ahhhhhhhhh."

His friend stopped chasing Harold and said, "What is it, man?"

"A ghost just threw a potion in my face. It burns. Oh, it burns," he yelled as he rubbed his face with his hands.

"You fool, there is no such thing as ghosts."

While the second griefer's attention was distracted by his friend's howls of pain, Otis and Bob snuck behind the second griefer. They placed a TNT block – extracted from one of Otis's many traps – just behind him and then slowly backed away.

Once they had reached a safe distance from the TNT, Otis yelled, "Hey."

The griefer turned around and said, "A pigman jockey? What are you doing here?"

Otis shrugged. "Just this," he said as he flipped a lever in his hands.

When the griefer saw the lever, he looked down and noticed the TNT block. But before he could react, the block exploded, burying the griefer under tons of cobblestone rubble.

The explosion was deafening. My ears were ringing. I was a little too close to the explosion and I felt dizzy.

"What is going on?" yelled the other griefer, still rubbing his eyes and moaning with pain from the harming potion.

"We are freeing our friends," I mumbled, coughing dust out of my undead lungs.

The griefer slumped down to the ground and started crying. I ignored him.

The explosion had covered my invisible body with dust, and Harold saw my dusty form stumbling around. He bumped me from behind and said, "Get on, Zeke. We have to free Zeb."

I was grateful for the ride.

Harold trotted over to where the ten zombies were still chained.

The explosion had knocked the unsuspecting zombies to the ground, but they were all still alive ... or ... still undead.

I dismounted from Harold and kneeled by Zeb. "Zeb, are you hurt?"

Zeb looked where my head should have been and saw nothing but a dust-covered body. His eyes grew wide with fear. "Ahhhhhhh, stay away from me, baby ghost," he shouted.

"Zeb, it's Zeke. I drank a potion of invisibility," I said. "See, Harold's right there."

Zeb looked over at Harold. He breathed a sigh of relief.

"Hi, Zeb," said Harold.

"Wow, am I glad to see you guys. I was getting really weak. Those griefers have been working me to death since they captured me yesterday."

I stood up and grabbed a pickaxe from off the ground. "Look out," I said to Zeb as I started smashing the axe against the iron chain on his leg. I was able to break it in just a few hits.

Zeb rubbed his leg where the chain had been. "Thanks," said Zeb.

Otis grabbed another pickaxe, and we quickly freed the other nine zombies.

"Come on," said Otis. "We need to get out of here. That potion of harming will wear off soon, and that other griefer might have survived the blast."

Otis mounted Bob and the two led the way out of the mine pit with the nine freed zombies following behind. Zeb waited with me to bring up the rear of the line.

"Thanks for freeing me, Zeke," said Zeb, putting his hand on my head.

"You would have done it for me," I said.

Zeb smiled. "Zeke, I think the potion is wearing off. I can see you again."

I looked down at my arms. Sure enough, I could see the rotten green color of my skin slowly reappearing.

The other zombies had left the mine pit, and it was time for Zeb and me to follow.

I looked behind me one more time to check that the griefer was still sitting on the ground crying, but he was gone!

Chapter 8

"Zeb, that other griefer is gone," I whispered.

Zeb looked to the empty space where the griefer had been. "Maybe he just ran away," Zeb suggested.

I shook my head. "I doubt it. Those guys were evil. Evil players always want revenge."

Zeb did not disagree with me.

"Look, Zeb, let's get out of here and warn the others. We

need to get to the surface as quickly as possible."

I jumped on Harold and ran ahead, with Zeb following. We soon caught up with the zombie line and warned everyone. Otis and Bob moved as quickly as they could without leaving the weak, ambling zombies behind.

Incredibly, we made it all the way back to the entrance to the main chamber without encountering the griefer.

"Wow," said Otis, "I can't believe the missing griefer didn't attack us."

"Yeah, I thought we'd have to battle him," I said, breathing a sigh of relief. "And, that would not have been pretty."

We all walked into the main chamber and collapsed from fatigue. I pulled out some wheat grains and put them in a pile for Harold and Bob. They eagerly pecked the seed. I pulled out some cooked meat and passed it around to the zombies.

Then, I walked over to Zeb and gave him a piece. He looked at me and said, "Thank you, Zeke. You are a great zombie."

I smiled. "Sure, Zeb. I owe you a lot. You've always been nice to me."

Suddenly we heard an evil laugh coming from across the chamber, and then, "Awww, isn't that cute?"

We looked in the direction of the sound and saw the griefer standing in front of the exit leading to the outside world.

The other zombies cowered in fear, but not me, not Otis and not Zeb.

"Where is your friend?" asked Otis, taunting the griefer. "Still under a few tons of rock?"

"Actually, I'm over here," said another evil voice.

We all turned around and saw the other griefer step out from behind a pile of rubble. He waved his diamond sword at us menacingly.

"What are you going to do to us?" asked one of the zombies.

"You? You only have to be a slave again," said the griefer blocking the chamber's exit. "But we are going to kill those jockeys."

I was looking around, trying to figure out how we could escape. The only exit was back where we came from, and if we went down there, the griefers would easily catch us in the narrow passage. The only other exit was blocked by the griefers. We would have to fight.

Apparently Zeb had figured this out already because he shuffled over to me and whispered, "Zeke, I'll go for the griefer at the door. When he attacks me, do your best to defeat him."

"No, Zeb, he will kill you."

Zeb sighed. "I know, but I have lived a long undead life,

and I want to try and help you to do the same."

A tear welled up in my eye and ran down my face. "No, Zeb, you can't."

"It's okay," said Zeb, patting me on the head.

Otis walked over. "Quit your sniveling, you baby. I've got a plan."

"What?" I asked.

"You'll know it when you see it," said Otis confidently.

"Hey," said one of the griefers, "what are you freaks talking about."

And that was when Otis yelled, "Now, Bob!"

A second later, the ground on which the two griefers were standing erupted with a massive explosion. The force of the explosion knocked everyone to the ground.

The first explosion was followed by a series of explosions that progressively blew a larger hole all the way to the outside world.

When the explosions stopped, we could see the night sky where before there had been only the inside of a mountain.

Where the griefers had been standing, there was a massive hole. It was so deep, we could see lava seeping in through the bottom.

"No way they survived that," said Zeb.

"They are dead for sure," I agreed. Then I turned to Otis. "How did you do that?"

"Didn't I tell you I had TNT traps everywhere?" said Otis proudly.

"Yeah, you did, but I never suspected this," I said.

"You're welcome," said Otis.

Chapter 9

We picked our way through the rubble and out to the grassland. Since it was night time, the adult zombies did not catch fire.

"Now what?" I said.

"We need to find a new place to spend the day," said Zeb.

"You could stay in the remains of this cave?" I suggested.

Zeb shook his head. "No, I'm sure more griefers will come back. It is not safe here."

"The old man's right," said Otis. "We need to find another place."

"We?" I said.

"Yeah," said Otis. "I like you. You are brave and smart. People who aren't brave and smart don't survive for long in this world."

"You are right about that," I said.

"I hate to interrupt this love festival," said Zeb, "but we only have a couple hours of night left.

We need to find shelter from the sun."

"Okay then," I said as I got on Harold's back. "Let's go find a new home."

End of Book 2

Can you help me?

Hi! Thank you so much for reading this book. Before you get a copy of Book 3, can you spare a moment to **leave a review** of this book where you bought it?

It's the best way for me to find out what you think about it. I think I'm doing a good job, but can't really know unless you leave reviews, so please leave one.

Thanks!

More Books

I've written dozens of *Baby Zeke* and other Minecraft-themed books. Just check any online retailer for a list of titles.

If you want to be alerted when I release a new book, be sure to **sign up for my email list** at *www.drblockbooks.com* or follow any of my social media platforms. I'm on Facebook, Twitter, and Instagram under @drblockbooks. I am also on

Goodreads, just search for "Dr. Block." I recommend signing up for the newsletter because you will get **TWO FREE**, *subscriber-exclusive short stories* as well as a periodic newsletter.

Yours Truly,
Dr. Block

Have you read my other unofficial Minecraft stories?

AN UNOFFICIAL MINECRAFT BOOK

DIARY OF A

SURFER VILLAGER

1

DR. BLOCK

CRAFT YOUR
OWN ADVENTURE

THE DEEPEST CAVE

DR.BLOCK AN UNOFFICIAL
MINECRAFT BOOK

AN UNOFFICIAL MINECRAFT BOOK

CREEP
TASTIC

DR. BLOCK

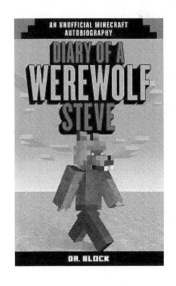

AN UNOFFICIAL MINECRAFT
AUTOBIOGRAPHY

DIARY OF A
WEREWOLF
STEVE

DR. BLOCK

About the Author

I, Dr. Block, believe that Minecraft is the greatest game ever created, mainly because it has the most awesome characters and mobs ever created. I have been studying all the mobs and have worked with the most interesting of them to create and publish their autobiographies. I am already working on more for you to read so you can learn about the amazing world that is Minecraft.

Stay tuned!

Made in the USA
Las Vegas, NV
02 December 2024

13201417R00053